Turn the dial each time a child falls out of bed

Child's Play (International) Ltd
© 1979 M. Twinn   ISBN 085953 095 7
Printed in Singapore

There were **9** in the bed

"Roll over
roll over"

So they all rolled over
and
one
fell out

There were **8** in the bed

"Roll over
roll over"

So they all rolled over
and
one
fell out

There were **7** in the bed

"Roll over
roll over"

So they all rolled over
and
one
fell out

There were **6** in the bed

"Roll over
roll over"

So they all rolled over
and
one
fell out

There were **5** in the bed

"Roll over
roll over"

So they all rolled over
and
one
fell out

There were **4** in the bed

"Roll over
roll over"

So they all rolled over
and
one
fell out

There were **3** in the bed

"Roll over
roll over"

So they all rolled over
and
one
fell out

There were **2** in the bed

"Roll over
roll over"

So they all rolled over
and
one
fell out

There was **1** in the bed

"Roll over
roll over"

So he rolled over
and
he
fell out

There were none in the bed

"Good night"